GRIMBLE at CHRISTMAS

GRIMBLE AT CHRISTMAS
A JONATHAN CAPE BOOK 978 0 224 08368 3

Published in Great Britain by Jonathan Cape,
an imprint of Random House Children's Books
A Random House Group Company

First published by Puffin Books 1974
This edition published 2008

1 3 5 7 9 10 8 6 4 2

Set in 12/14.5pt Adobe Caslon by Falcon Oast Graphic Art Ltd.

RANDOM HOUSE CHILDREN'S BOOKS
61–63 Uxbridge Road, London W5 5SA

www.kidsatrandomhouse.co.uk
www.rbooks.co.uk

Addresses for companies within The Random House Group Limited can be found at:
www.randomhouse.co.uk/offices.htm

THE RANDOM HOUSE GROUP Limited Reg. No. 954009

A CIP catalogue record for this book is available from the British Library.

Printed and bound in Great Britain by Clays Ltd, St Ives plc

The Random House Group Limited supports the Forest Stewardship Council (FSC),
the leading international forest certification organization. All our titles that are
printed on Greenpeace-approved FSC-certified paper carry the FSC logo.
Our paper procurement policy can be found at www.rbooks.co.uk/environment.

GRIMBLE
at
CHRISTMAS

CLEMENT FREUD

Illustrated by Quentin Blake

Jonathan Cape

To my grandchildren especially

Alexandra, Tom, Jack, Martha, Harry, Max,

Nicholas, Joshua, Sophie, Scarlett, Jake, Charlie,

Spike, Gorge, Jonah, Charlotte and Samson

Contents

1. Seven Shopping Days to Christmas

Grimble's parents were very forgetful. This was sometimes annoying, but having a forgetful father and mother also had advantages. For instance it meant that he had better bedtimes than most other children. Quite often he used to go into his father's room and say, "I'm going to bed now; it's midnight," and his father would say, "Don't wait up for me," or "Iquique is the only town I know with two qs!"

For most of the year Grimble – Grimble was his whole name, his parents had forgotten to give him any other names – rather enjoyed having a father and mother who were different from those of the other boys at school, but when it came to Christmas there were very definite disadvantages.

Grimble had only two more days of school before the Christmas holidays started – and the old

Grimbles went around as if it were the middle of February or the end of August; anyway there was nothing special about the way they went around. The shops in the High Street had windows decorated with lights and Father Christmases and wrapped-up packages and mince pies and a big notice saying ONLY SEVEN MORE SHOPPING DAYS TO CHRISTMAS on which the number of days before the twenty-fifth was changed every evening . . . it was very exciting.

And Grimble's mother went out with a big shopping bag – and came back with a cabbage, and one and a half pounds of cod fillets. I don't want to be unkind about cod fillets. They are perfectly all right but they just do not make you tingle all over. Anyway they didn't make Grimble tingle all over.

Grimble had a friend called David Sebastian Waghorn whose mother had said, "We are going to have cold turkey on Boxing Day." That is just about the same as saying, "On Christmas Day, we are going to have hot roast turkey with stuffing and gravy and sausages and bacon and roast potatoes and Brussels sprouts." He waited anxiously for Mrs Grimble to give some small hint like that. The evening before she had said, "We haven't got a cat," and Mrs Grimble said, "Oh dear nor we have, don't forget to leave her a saucer of milk."

Grimble watched his parents carefully for any sign that they might have remembered why he was going to be on holiday and when, and what sort of treats he was going to get if he was going to get treats. He worked hard giving them well-mannered hints because it was terribly important to him that Christmas would be, well . . . complete.

One evening he dropped a lot of pine needles on the carpet . . . but as no one noticed or said anything and Grimble was very tidy, he got a dustpan and brush and swept them up again a couple of days later.

Also he tried to hum "Good King Wenceslaus" . . . mm mmmmmmmm mm mmmmmm m but he did not hum very well and his father thinking it was "God Save The Queen," stood up and when Grimble had finished humming his father turned off the television set and went to bed.

So he practised humming some more. David Sebastian Waghorn had a joke about humming. "Do you know why humming birds hum? Because they don't know the words." Grimble thought David Sebastian Waghorn was a very funny boy.

The day before, Mr Grimble had come into the house with a large square parcel and Grimble, knowing that it was not polite to be openly curious, had gone into the kitchen and watched his father take the parcel into the study through the slightly open door. It looked as if it might be a bicycle taken to pieces or a large box kite or possibly a new kind of cooker.

That evening his father said, "Come into the study and see what I've got in my parcel. It's a foot-stool, I gave it to me..." and Grimble had clenched his teeth and said, "Now you can lie back in your chair and don't even have to bend your legs." His father was delighted that Grimble had got the point of the footstool so quickly and showed him where Iquique was on the globe of the world . . . it was about halfway down South America on the left-hand side.

"Do you expect to get anything else for Christmas . . . except for my presents . . ." he asked his father in an offhand way. "A lot of weather," said his father who had just found Birmingham on the globe.

That night when Grimble was in bed he started to think about Christmas very seriously. Christmas was a holiday and a time for eating interesting food and giving presents and receiving presents – someone had told him that it was more blessed to do one than the other, but he kept forgetting which. Now the reason why children expected their parents to do things for them at Christmas was because parents are better organized than children and parents have more money than children.

In Grimble's case this was only partly true. His parents were not nearly as well organized as he; they kept forgetting to get up in the morning and sometimes forgot to go to bed for days on end and they never knew what time it was.

But the old Grimbles did have more money than

he . . . or he hoped they did, because Grimble only had 19p and an Irish 5p piece. He lay in bed practicing his humming and wondering whether, if one was really well organized, as he was – satchel packed; homework done; toothpaste squeezed out on to toothbrush; tie tied in a knot and opened out into a big loop so that it would go over his head; shoelaces done up so that he could step into his shoes and wriggle them about till the heels gave way . . . anyway, if someone were really well organized, it should not be very difficult for him to make money . . . and if he had money then he could arrange the whole family Christmas celebrations.

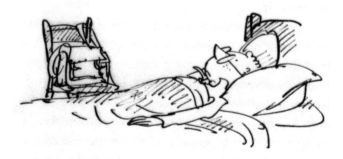

One evening Grimble had listened to a television programme about money in which a man had said that the important thing was to find something that everyone needed. That way, you had a ready market for whatever you were going to sell . . . for instance the man explained: "It is a better thing to go from house to house selling socks, which everyone wears, than suspenders – which are rubber straps that go round your leg below the knee and keep the socks up. Hardly anyone wears suspenders," said the man. Grimble had never even heard of suspenders. "Also," said the man, "you have to spend some of your money on getting people interested in your wares – this is called advertising."

Grimble was very impressed and wrote a small note to remind himself: to sell successfully you have to find something everyone wants, and advertise it.

It was quite clear to Grimble that if a man wants to earn money by selling things, he would have to buy them first; the simple problem that Grimble had was what could he buy for 19p that he might be able to sell for a lot of money – because a turkey and a Christmas pudding and presents and everything would cost pounds. One of the masters at school had told them about an old Greek who was lying in a bathtub when an apple fell on his head and he shouted, "Eureka, I've got it!" and invented gold, or something like that. Grimble lay in his bed thinking hard waiting to shout, "Eureka, I've got it!" but he fell asleep.

In the morning he went to the shop on the corner and as it was empty he looked carefully around for something that everyone needed that cost 19p or less. There were rolls of flypaper and some suntan cream and washing soap and tins of sardines and lemonade crystals. These were all dusty, which is a bad sign. Suddenly he saw a loaf of bread and a great idea occurred to him: everyone needed bread; if he went around selling bread slice by slice to people so that they wouldn't have to go to shops he could become very rich. And then he thought most people already have bread, but if I sold toast . . . not only sold it but took it to people just when they wanted it. When they were sitting at the breakfast table with butter on the knife and a marmalade jar in front of them . . . THE GRIMBLE HOME TOAST DELIVERY SERVICE. PROPRIETOR GRIMBLE. "Eureka, I've got it!" he shouted and the old lady came out from the back of the shop and said, "If you've got it you'd better pay for it. That is the only way you can do things in a shop."

Grimble was much too excited to explain, so he paid the lady 6p which was the price of that loaf of bread and went to school.

He didn't learn much at school that day because he was working out his toast business. The loaf of bread was in his locker; it was a cut loaf called THIN SLICED which seemed a silly name to give a loaf and it contained eighteen pieces of bread wrapped in greaseproof paper. (If the business really succeeds he thought, I might go into the greaseproof-paper business.)

Every morning nearly everyone eats toast and, as toast is quite boring to make, Grimble decided that if he made toast at seven every morning and brought it to people all hot and ready they would definitely pay 2½p for three slices, which meant six times three slices in a loaf which is 15p back for 6p.

When he came home from school he sat down at his desk and got a large piece of paper and cut it in half and then cut each half into half again and then halved the four pieces of paper so that he had eight small pieces and on each one he wrote the message THE GRIMBLE HOME TOAST DELIVERY SERVICE. PROPRIETOR GRIMBLE founded 1974. On the other side he wrote: Toast delivered, daily, tidily, un-burnedly, punctually. 2½p for three slices. Our representative will call tomorrow morning with a free slice and awaits the pleasure of your order.

He took the eight pieces of paper and put four of them through the letter boxes of the four houses up the hill from his house and posted the other four through the doors on the downhill side. As he was going back home he decided that as he did not know a great deal about toast he had better go and see Madame Beryl, who was a fat kind friend of his mother's who kept a bakery shop and knew a lot about things like that.

"Good afternoon," said Grimble, entering the shop. "I would like to have a small discussion with you about bread." "I prefer," said Madame Beryl, "to talk about cake." "I meant to say toast," said Grimble. "I still meant cake," said Madame Beryl. She eased her right foot out of her shoe, which came away with a small sigh of relief, and said, "I would very much like to talk to you about bread *and* toast but unfortunately I have to go and see a man about a wedding breakfast. Can it wait until after Christmas?"

"I am afraid," said Grimble, "that after Christmas will be exactly too late." There was a small silence. "I have done a very silly thing," said Madame Beryl. "I baked a cake which had not been ordered and now I don't know what to do with it and the dustbin is full. Do you think you would be very kind and take possession of it?" "Oh, yes, thank you," said Grimble, "if it is really in your way." And Madame Beryl put her foot back into her protesting shoe, got a quite large cake, gave it to Grimble, said, "Oh dear, I must fly," and started moving into the street like a cabin trunk. "About toast," said Grimble following her. "Not toast," puffed Madame Beryl. "Never toast cake. Ice it with icing sugar and egg white," and she waddled onto a bus.

Grimble found himself alone with a cake and then he thought, actually a cake with icing is a very Christmassy thing to have and tomorrow I shall start up my business and in nine days' time it will be Christmas Eve and even if my parents have forgotten, it's going to be an absolutely complete proper well-organized Christmas.

2. Home Toast
Delivery

The next morning Grimble woke early. He had not slept very well owing to his business problems. His assets, with Christmas Eve eight days away, were one iced cake hidden in a cupboard, 13p in a money box, the Irish 5p piece and a wrapped loaf of which he had reckoned to give away eight slices in the cause of advertising.

The old Grimbles had a toaster with two slots in it and the idea was that you put in two slices of bread . . . and after a minute and a bit they would pop up, done to a turn.

What really happened was that after the allotted time the toaster gave a small whirring noise and a click and you had to get a knife or a fork or a spoon and prise out the bread which had got stuck. Looking at the situation calmly, Grimble realized that the toast industry was going to be something of a gamble until he had a full list of cash clients and was able to buy efficient machinery for the production of high-class wares.

The next morning he got up about seven o'clock, took eight paper napkins and wrote on each of them, "With the compliments of G.H.T.D.S." This meant the Grimble Home Toast Delivery Service; putting the initials was much quicker than writing out the words. He then counted out eight slices of bread, wrapped the remaining slices firmly in the greaseproof paper so that they would stay fresh, and decided to make the toast two slices at a time . . . because, being the first day he would have to stay and talk about money and delivery time. When things got organized he might be able to throw slices of toast straight through the letter boxes . . . provided the people did not have dogs or cats or mice.

At a quarter past seven he turned on the toaster, and put in two slices and as soon as they were ready he prised them out, wrapped them in the paper napkin and ran out of the house. He started at the two houses just up the hill from his; they were absolutely dark. No lights, nothing. He wondered whether there might be some money to be made out of The Grimble Reliable Morning Alarm

Service – but decided that having invested so large a part of his capital in the toast business, he had better concentrate on that.

He went up to the first house and rang the bell; as nothing happened and the toast was certainly not getting any hotter he rang it again and knocked. After a while the lights in the house went on and a man opened the door.

"Good morning," said Grimble. "I bring you toast on behalf of the Grimble Home Toast Delivery Service. I expect you received my literature," and he gave the man his best smile and the free slice of toast. The man looked at it with appreciation. It was well-toasted toast. "Oh yes," said the man. "G.H.T.D.S. come in."

Grimble went into the house and the man said, "Sit down. Good idea this toast delivery. The wife and I would like to join but we don't have breakfast. Can we use it for lunch?"

"I am afraid," said Grimble, "that as yet I have no lunch toast service, but if I may, I will enter your name and call again when such a service commences."

He said goodbye and went to the next house. He rang the bell and waited and finally saw a man and a woman through the glass of the front door, the man with a walking stick and the woman, making little twitty whimpering noises, saying, "Harold don't be so angry it might be the postman with a new 4p delivery that comes earlier than the 3p one . . . or possibly it is last week's 3½p letters come at last.'

"It's Grimble," shouted Grimble through the letter box. "the Grimble Toast Delivery Service."

"Bless my boots," said the man. "It's the breakfast toast," and he opened the door and asked Grimble to come in. "Good morning, sir," said Grimble. "I do hope you received my letter." The man said yes he had. "Here," said Grimble, "is your free slice of toast with the compliments of the directors of the company.'

The man unwrapped it and ate it quietly.

"Excellent," he said. "First class piece of toast. Congratulate you!" "Thank you, sir," said Grimble. "I'll take the service," said the man. "Three slices a day, eight o'clock prompt. Pay on Friday, start the day after Christmas. We're going away to shoot salmon in Scotland this afternoon. Nice to have met you."

"After Christmas," Grimble muttered. "That's not going to help buy a turkey" – and he rushed home to make the next two slices, wondering why he was not feeling as happy as he had been earlier that morning. His parents were still asleep, the toaster was ready and in a very short time he had the new supply of toast and was at the house downhill from his own. As he went up the path a man opened the door and said, "Aha come on in, been waiting for my toast," and he took his free sample slice from Grimble's hand, buttered it, put marmalade on it and said, "There." Then he said, "There," two more times. Grimble wondered "where" but decided that customers were always right, said nothing and waited. "Good," said the man. "A bit too much butter but that may have been my fault. I'll take the service, every day . . . but I would prefer brown toast. All right?"

Brown toast. No toast. Toast after Christmas . . . Grimble said, "Thank you, I shall let you know, at present the service is confined to white, thin, sliced which is the popular demand," and went next door.

This time it was a woman who answered the door. Grimble preferred men. "Hello," said the woman, "you've come about the toast." Grimble admitted this. "How old are you?" asked the woman. (This was really why Grimble preferred men.) "About ten," he said. "Oh," said the woman, "how nice, I have a little nephew who is coming for Christmas. He is nine and three quarters, you must come and meet him." There was a short silence. "Excuse me," said Grimble, "how old are you?" The woman looked slightly put out and said, "What an extraordinary thing for a small boy to ask." Then she gave an embarrassed giggle and said, "I-am-in-my-middle-thirties," all in one gasp. "How nice," said Grimble, "I have a mother at home who is in her middle thirties. I do hope you will be able to come round sometime and play with her. We live two houses up the hill. Now about the toast." "Ah yes," said the woman, "Toast. Actually we make our own toast."

"I realize this," said Grimble. "But the point of the service is that we take the hard work out of toast for you at a very modest charge, 2¹/₂p for three slices." The woman looked at Grimble and thought some more and finally said, "May I sleep on it?" "I would not advise it," said Grimble. "Sleeping on toast may well keep it warm but it would do nothing to keep it crisp and fresh."

"I mean I would like to think about it tonight . . ." said the woman, and Grimble remembering his good manners said, "Naturally, Madam; our aim is to please," and left the house.

When he got home his mother was up making toast with *his* bread. This was very unusual . . . I mean for his mother to be up was very unusual – and Grimble took four of the slices of toast his mother had made and, very quickly, because it was getting quite near his school time, he raced round the four remaining houses that he had warned of the toast service. He slipped the toast through the letterboxes, shouted, "Will try to come back this evening," and ran home.

"Where have you been?" asked Mrs Grimble, her head inside the refrigerator. "Out," said Grimble, and realizing that this was not a very complete reply added, "actually feeding

18

under-privileged people." His father had told him once that when people began a sentence with "actually", it was nearly always a lie. His mother, who had not been listening, said, "Here is your breakfast. Come home straight from school, because we are going shopping."

"Shopping," said Grimble; "Christmas shopping and there are still six shopping days to go . . ." "Well," said his mother, "actually mostly going to the launderette and things."

Grimble drank his glass of iced milk which his mother had finally taken out of the refrigerator and went to school. She said "actually", said Grimble to himself. That means she was telling a lie. It *is* Christmas shopping.

Walking to school he thought about the eight slices of bread given away and the rest probably eaten by the old Grimbles. I don't know how anyone can make a living in this country. It's the fault of the Government. When I grow up I am going to be a Government. Then anyone with a good idea will be able to make a lot of money . . .

That afternoon, when he returned from school, his father said, "Some people called and left you some toast . . . hold on I'll find it. I looked at it carefully and there was no messages in it. Just toast wrapped in a napkin with some initials on it ... I wonder what it can mean." "Actually," said Grimble "it's a new club" ... and blushed. It was the second lie he had told that day. His father went out and brought back three slices of toast still wrapped with the G.H.T.D.S. slip on them and just then his mother called, "Come on, Grimble," and they went shopping. Grimble's idea of shopping was to go into a shop, find something he wanted, and say, "I'll buy it." Mrs Grimble did not work like that. She went into a shop, found something she liked and then spent the next half hour looking at a lot of things similar to it, that she didn't mind, to make sure she liked the first thing she had seen as much as she thought she had liked it when she first saw it. This wasted a lot of time and was very weary for their feet.

After his mother had bought a few womanish things made out of buckles and elastic they went into a food shop. Grimble headed straight for the turkey counter and looked with interest at the turkeys. His mother bought lemons. So Grimble, watching his mother out of the corner of his eye, stood in front of the Christmas puddings and as

Mrs Grimble moved off to the tomato-ketchup shelf he said, "Oh look . . . Christmas puddings for small families. What a good idea. I thought you could only buy enormous ones."

"Heavy things Christmas puddings," said his mother. "Make you feel tired – like eating hedgehogs. You go and wait for me at the launderette.'

Grimble left his mother in the food store and went to the launderette and watched the clothes go round. It was a bit like colour television only even less plot.

He was just getting interested in a green shirt which was twisting itself affectionately around a pair of white underpants, when his mother came in with a large parcel and said, "Come *on*, Grimble, let's go home."

Grimble took one corner of the parcel and his mother took the other and they carried it home and on the way back he said to his mother, very casually, "Tell me . . . what would be a good thing to do with three slices of stale toast?" His mother was a very surprising woman. Most mothers would have said, "throw them away", or else pretend not to have heard; not Mrs Grimble. She put down the parcel, sat on the pavement, and said, "Three pieces of stale toast. I know exactly what you can do. You can make welsh rarebit with some cheese and an egg and some mustard, if you like mustard, and I shall pay you 2p for every welsh rarebit you make."

Grimble looked at Mrs Grimble and thought, she really is quite a splendid woman. Three times 2p are exactly 6p, which is what I lost on my thin sliced loaf . . . and at home there is a very good book on cooking. It will tell me all about welsh rabbits.

3. Four Shopping Days
to Christmas

*N*ow there were only four more proper shopping days to Christmas. Father Grimble was in the study looking at some very small islands on the globe through his microscope . . . which is a machine that makes small things look bigger. Mother Grimble was in bed with her feet and Grimble was on holiday. That morning he had had his first proper holiday feeling; first he did not get up and then he quite especially did not go to school and at nine o'clock there was no roll call, and he didn't answer his name. He purposely did not have milk at eleven, although he would have quite liked a glass, and then they had lunch.

Grimble cooked. A bag of potato crisps, peanut-butter sandwiches with chutney, a tin of baked beans, a 2½p piece of fudge and a bottle of fizzy lemonade with two straws. Grimble did not understand how anyone drank out of a lemonade bottle with less than two straws and as straws are very cheap – eighty-three straws cost the same as a bottle of lemonade – it was just meanness when people gave you a single one.

The best thing about Grimble's lunch was the washing up. There was hardly any, and he left it for his mother to do when she felt better.

A very odd thing happened after lunch. You know how you can go weeks and weeks without getting a letter and then suddenly get two? Well, after lunch the postman came and there were three letters, all for Grimble. Three letters – although one was in a brown envelope.

He took them up to his bedroom and opened them carefully. The first was from his Aunt Percy. He knew because she had funny handwriting with words underlined.

As he opened it he thought he noticed a one-pound note lurking just inside the flap, but he read the letter first . . .

Dear Grimble, here is one <u>pound</u>
for <u>Christmas</u>. I shall take <u>cat</u> away
to the sea for a few days. We shall
probably go <u>by</u> bus.
Your loving
Aunt <u>Persimmon</u>

He took out his notebook, in which there was
a page at the end headed CASH, and crossed out
19p and wrote 119p; then he thought, I have not
been very clever and he rubbed out the 119 and
put in a 1 in front of the 19. There. One should
be able to get a jolly decent Christmas tree for

119p *and* have a bit left over for some washing-up powder, which was going to be his Christmas present for his mother.

The second letter was from David Sebastian Waghorn.

DEAR GRIM,

WILL YOU COME AND SPEND THE DAY WITH US ON THURSDAY? IF WE DO NOT HEAR FROM YOU, I SHALL EXPECT YOU AFTER BREAKFAST. IF YOU CANNOT COME, COME AFTER BREAKFAST AND EXPLAIN WHY. DSW.

David Sebastian Waghorn *was* a very funny boy.

So Grimble, feeling quite particularly cheerful, opened the last letter; the one that was in the brown envelope. It had not even been stuck down, and said: "Dear Sir or Madam," which Grimble thought not a very polite way to start a letter.

You are probably going to get very fat at Christmas. All those rich foods washed down with important wine followed by heavy puddings covered in cream and brandy butter and old cheese and biscuits and things like that. Well, we at Thumpyew Farm are ready for you. We give you orange juice and hot water flavoured with just a teeny bit of lemon and on Sundays you get two peeled grapes, and in hardly any time at all you will regain your youth and your health and your figure. Just think about it as you stuff roast turkey into yourself next week. We at Thumpyew are ready and willing to help YOU get THIN . . .

And it gave an address to which one could reply.

Now I wonder why they chose me, thought Grimble. He opened the door of a cupboard that had a mirror attached to it and stood in front of it, sideways with his shirt tucked under his chin. Well, his back was certainly thinner than his tummy. I mean, his back sort of caved in while his tummy stuck out, but surely not as far as that. Anyway how did Thumpyew know he was going to stuff himself with turkey and things? Unless he did something about it, the chances were that on Christmas Day he was going to get fish fingers.

He put the pound note into his wallet slipped the three letters under his pillow and went out. In the shopping street there was a greengrocer called Flewett who sold Christmas trees. A Christmas tree, Grimble decided, was absolutely completely essential to Christmas, and he stood in front of the shop looking at a notice which said 20p a foot. He was just wondering what people could do with an extra foot (win a 3-legged race by oneself?) when he realized that it did not mean a foot with five toes at the end and a shoe on the outside, but a foot with twelve inches to it.

So for 8op he could buy a four-foot tree, and as he had 119p he would still have 39p left to buy something for 40p with 1p off for his mother. He peered through the shop window and saw someone peering out at him and he waved; and the person who was looking out waved, so he smiled and the person smiled back. It was a boy with glasses and freckles and suddenly he recognized him. It was a boy from his class. He looked closely at him and said, "Grimble" (for it was he) "you are definitely getting a little fat." Thumpyew was right. "Now that you are on holiday you are not taking enough exercise", and he started hopping around outside the shop, watching himself in the shop window and wondering whether he was suddenly going to get thinner or whether it took a long time.

As he was hopping around the greengrocer came out and said, "Excuse me, are you all right?" Grimble said, "Yes. I'm just taking a little exercise." Mr Flewett looked at him and said, "If it's exercise you want you can do some delivering for me; Christmas trees; I pay according to the length of tree. You look a good strong boy. You can take this three-foot tree to stationmaster Wheeler at the station for 5p."

"Oh thank you," said Grimble. "I know Mr Wheeler," and he took the tree and went off to the station.

He found that the best way of carrying the tree was folding his hands in front of his tummy, getting Mr Flewett to put the trunk into them, and resting the top of the tree against his head. It was quite easy to carry that way, although people in the street thought he was a Christmas tree on legs and some of them ran to the other side of the road.

Mr Wheeler was very pleased to see Grimble with his tree and gave him a free platform ticket and they went on to the platform and there was a weighing machine. "I wonder," Grimble asked, "whether I might weigh myself on your machine?" Mr Wheeler said, "Yes of course you can, and you need not put in a penny. I have the key," and he opened up the machine at the back and pressed a lever. There was a click and Grimble stood on the machine and he weighed just under five stone. As he got off the machine a card popped out of a slot and it had YOUR FORTUNE written on it. His fortune was a small card with printing:

BEWARE OF STRANGERS WITH BLACK HAIR. YOU ARE GOING ON A JOURNEY. THIS IS A GOOD TIME FOR LOVE. MONEY WILL BE DIFFICULT TO FIND.

"I don't know any strangers with black hair," said Grimble, "What very peculiar advice." Mr Wheeler said the machine was very old and it only had two fortunes. The other said:

A HAPPY EVENT WILL TAKE PLACE SOON. SOMEONE YOU LOVE IS GOING ON A JOURNEY. BE VERY CAREFUL NOT TO GET TOO CLOSE TO WATER.

"That means if I weighed myself twice I would get both fortunes."

"That's right," said the stationmaster. "We like people to do that because of the 'journey' part. That way more people go on the railway."

Grimble went back to the shop and realized that he now had enough money to buy a six-foot tree ... if he didn't get any soap powder for his mother. A six-foot tree would be marvellous. Six foot was much bigger than he was. When he got back to the greengrocer, he decided to ask whether he might buy a tree for himself with a bit off the price for delivering it to himself, but as soon as Mr Flewett saw him he said, "Here you are. Take this four footer to Number 26, The Terrace; they've got a children's party with dancing-round-the-tree, and the tree isn't there yet." So Grimble took the tree and ran.

It was very heavy, but as he waddled along he said to himself, "Now we'll be able to get the biggest Christmas tree anywhere, especially if I get a special price for delivering my own tree."

When he got back there was only one tree left outside the shop. It was the biggest one of all and the greengrocer was waiting for Grimble and said, "That's my last tree; we'll have to take it between us because it's too big for one person to carry." Grimble said, "All right ... but will there be no more trees?"

"Not now," said Mr Flewett. "Trees are all finished now. We start selling tangerines after this."

Grimble was very sad. He liked tangerines but you can't put presents under a tangerine. You can't even put a lot of candles into a tangerine and light them. And there was not another Christmas-tree shop in the district. "Come on then," said the greengrocer, and he took the thick end and led the way. Grimble got hold of the trunk near the top and followed him down the street. It must have looked funny. The big greengrocer at the front end – and all you could see at the back was a pair of shoes under a lot of branches. "I can't see where I'm going," shouted Grimble towards the trunk.

"You just hold your end up," shouted the green-grocer over his shoulder. "I'll pull you in the right direction."

They walked a very long way and then he heard the man say, "Here we are, hold on," and he heard the trunk drop and a bell ring and a woman's voice saying, "Oh there it is, you'd better hide it in the shed in the garden because I don't want someone to see it just yet."

Grimble thought it was rather a nice voice, a bit like his mother's, and then the voice said, "Will you put it on my account please," and Mr Flewett said, "Certainly, Madam, goodbye," and the lady went back into the house and Grimble came out from the tree and looked up and it was his house. He had delivered the Christmas tree to his own house.

He helped Mr Flewett hide the tree in the shed and then he walked about for a few minutes – thinking. First he thought he must have managed to lose a little weight after all that exercise and that delivering Christmas trees was better than living on nothing but orange juice and peeled grapes.

And then he thought about his mother. She had said she didn't want "someone" to see the

Christmas tree and the only someone he could think of was himself. He decided he would pretend not to know about the tree so she wouldn't be upset. Really he was very pleased – it was one less thing for him to organize.

Then he went inside. "There you are," said his mother. "Did you have a nice day?" "Yes thank you," said Grimble. "Are your feet better?" His mother said they were a bit better but she was going to bed and if it was not too much trouble could she have some fudge.

As Grimble had never made fudge, he said that might take a little time, but his mother said that didn't matter. "I have plenty of time now because there is nothing else to do, is there?"

"I hope not," said Grimble and went off to find a book called *How to Make Fudge and Other Good Tricks*.

4. David Sebastian Waghorn

It was now Thursday and Grimble had arranged to spend the day with his friend David Sebastian Waghorn. The Waghorns lived in a large house, which was built a very short time ago but tried to look old.

Mr Waghorn was a loud man who shouted a lot. The odd thing was that he did not only shout when he was angry, the way most people do; he shouted all the time.

"HELLO, GRIMBLE," he shouted. "HERE'S, GRIMBLE," and then he raised his voice and shouted, "GRIMBLE IS HERE."

So Grimble said, "Good morning, Mr Waghorn. I am here."

"RECOGNIZED YOU," shouted Mr Waghorn, "KNEW WHO YOU WERE. MUST GO TO WORK. GOODBYE," and then in case everyone had not heard him he shouted it again: "GOODBYE."

Mrs Waghorn was a small quiet lady with blue hair. Not bright blue but a pastel shade, which some hairdressers think is nice. She was very kind to people, to make up for her husband shouting so loudly.

Mrs Waghorn liked washing up better than anything and, when Grimble and David Sebastian Waghorn had stood for a minute or two whispering to each other, she put on some rubber gloves and went off to do the dishes with a lovely smile on her face.

Grimble and David Sebastian Waghorn went off to the sitting room to inspect a new book called *Party Tricks*, which Mr Waghorn had given his son as a non-birthday present. They lay on the floor and started to look for something which, the book promised, would "confuse and delight friends and family".

One of the best tricks in the book was: Take a pack of cards which everyone will think is a real pack, but only you know that all the cards are queens of spades. Ask someone to pick a card, to look at it and put it back into the pack; then shuffle the cards, pretend to examine them carefully and take one from the pack. Naturally this will be the queen of spades. People will think you very clever.

"I wonder how often you can play that trick on the same person," Grimble said. "After you have shown someone a different queen of spades half a dozen times, I think they could get suspicious . . ."

"You know something," said Grimble. "There are fifty-two different cards in the pack. Suppose they are not all queens of spades but just ordinary cards and you went up to fifty-two different people and said, 'Take a card. Put it back. It was the queen of spades.' Unless you are terribly unlucky at least one of them will have taken the queen of spades and be very impressed and those who took one of the other queens will be fairly impressed. The rest of the people won't be very impressed. Do you think that is a good trick?"

"No," said David Sebastian Waghorn. "Actually the best sort of trick is when there are two of *us* against one of *them*. Suppose I give my mother a pack of cards from which she picks one and puts it back. You could be standing behind her as she looks at it and then you can signal to me and tell me what card she took."

"That is a very good idea indeed," said Grimble.

"If we worked hard on that we could go into business together as Grimble and Waghorn, Conjurers to the Nobility; and if things went well and we learned more than one trick we might appear on a Royal Variety Programme and be By Appointment Grimble and Waghorn."

"Or Waghorn and Grimble sounds quite nice," suggested David Sebastian Waghorn.

"I was taking the names in alphabetical order," said Grimble. "G comes before W."

"All right," said David Sebastian Waghorn, "let's practise our trick."

"Cards are either spades, hearts, diamonds or clubs – so when you see which card has been taken you signal; S is for spades and shirt so you point to your shirt. C is for clubs and collar. He is for heart and hair and D is for diamonds and . . . and . . . dustbin?"

"How are we going to find a dustbin?" asked Grimble.

"A very sensible remark," said David Sebastian Waghorn.

"What else begins with a D?"

After quite a lot of discussion they decided David Sebastian Waghorn began with a D, and if Grimble did the signalling he should point to David and if David did it he should point to himself, only be sure not to point to his hair, collar or shirt or the trick would go wrong.

When it came to actual cards, they decided to hold up fingers for the numbered cards – ace to ten and hold up the right fist for jack, the left fist for queen and both fists for king. They practised the trick for quite a long time before going into the kitchen to try it on Mrs Waghorn.

"I say," began Grimble, "I wonder whether you would like us to show you rather a clever trick."

Mrs Waghorn said she would like to see it, especially if she could do it without taking her washing-up gloves off.

"Well," said Grimble, "they are your cards but the trick would go better with bare hands."

So Mrs Waghorn took off her gloves and David Sebastian stood behind her and Grimble held out the pack and said, "Take a card. Look at it. Put it back. Now," said Grimble, "I am going to tell you what card it was."

David Sebastian Waghorn started signalling furiously. First he touched his nose, then he held up his right fist, then suddenly he changed his mind, pulled down his right fist and held up his left fist, and his mother turned around and said. "If you are going to hit me I shall be very angry and tell your father and you know what he will do."

"Shout," said David Sebastian Waghorn, quietly.

"Now," said Grimble, "let me tell you which card you picked. It was without very much shadow of doubt the queen of diamonds. Thank you, thank you, thank you."

"Oh dear," said Mrs Waghorn, "I seem to think it was the nine of spades but with all those wavings from David it is very hard to concentrate. Why don't you two boys go out into the garden with a football?" And the two boys went out in the garden with a football. David Sebastian Waghorn was very angry, "The trouble about my mother is that she has no card sense. It *was* the queen of diamonds."

Grimble thought they ought to forget about card tricks for the moment and start on football.

They began by putting down their jackets as goalposts and playing on the same side and every time they scored a goal they hugged each other the way footballers do on television. As there were no goalkeepers they scored a lot of goals and there was more hugging than football so they gave up and went back into the house and played psychiatrists; these are a special kind of doctor who do a lot of talking.

Grimble lay on the couch and David Sebastian Waghorn sat in a chair and said "Tell me now, Mr . . . err . . . Grimble did you say your name was . . . what appears to be the matter?"

"It's Christmas . . ." said Grimble. "I have got a cake and my mother has bought a heavy parcel and there is a Christmas tree hidden in the shed and I can do a pretty pathetic conjuring trick and is it going to be enough?"

"What do you expect from this – Christmas I think you call it, Mr, err, Grimble?"

"Well," said Grimble, "I expect rather a lot. Like a brown Windsor soup or at least a fairly brown Windsor soup. And then turkey and everything and Christmas pudding and things and crackers and balloons and all that. And a cake but I've got the cake."

David Sebastian Waghorn looked very serious and said, "You are suffering from Christmeasles and may have to have a Christmasectomy. I suggest you go into the garden and try to score a goal using your right foot. That will be seven pounds and fifty-five pence."

"There is another thing I'm worried about," said Grimble. "I do not have as much money as I would like to have."

"That," said David Sebastian Waghorn, "is much more serious. In fact I do not know when I heard of a more serious disease. Do your parents talk a lot about money?"

"No," said Grimble, "hardly ever."

"Then they have enough," said David. "Can you come back next week?"

"I could," said Grimble, "but it may be too late."

For lunch they had lamb chops cooked in breadcrumbs and spinach with mashed potatoes and then a chocolate pudding and in the afternoon Mrs Waghorn took them to the cinema and for all that time Grimble completely forgot about Christmas.

But after tea Grimble began thinking again and had another look at the party-trick book. Christmas had quite long gaps between meals and if there was nothing organized, which the old Grimbles were very good at ... I mean the old Grimbles were very good at not being organized, then it was up to Grimble to provide the entertainment.

There was quite a good trick in which you tucked a penny between your fingers and opened out your hand, and no one saw anything and then suddenly you had a penny in your hand. Grimble tried that trick a lot but finally the penny, which kept falling on the floor, rolled under the sofa, and he gave up.

Grimble left before Mr Waghorn came home – he decided he wasn't feeling strong enough to be shouted at – and when he got to his house he decided he needed something strengthening to eat, like fudge.

The night before, in his fudge book, he had read that you can make fudge of any flavour you like. Now onion was a flavour Grimble liked very much and he was sure it was strengthening. Onion fudge. The words had a sort of rightness about them. Onion fudge ... like strawberry jam or bacon sandwich.

Grimble put a saucepan on to the stove and then he found an onion and cut it in half and put it in the pan and then he went to look for some condensed milk. There was none in the larder and he couldn't find any in his father's study or in the bathroom where his mother might have left it – she used amazing things, like eggs, for washing her hair. Anyway there was no milk anywhere, but quite an interesting smell was coming from the kitchen.

He looked round and found it was coming from the saucepan . . . so he took it from the flame and when it was a bit cool he noticed that the onion had stuck to the bottom of the pan, because of the heat. By far the best way to unstick things that have burned on to pans is to pour on some water . . . so when the pan had cooled down he poured on some water and let it boil until the burned onion was loose and then, just before he threw away the water, he decided to taste it . . . he poured it into a cup, blew on it to make sure it was cool, and took a sip. It was not just golden coloured water. It was very good onion soup . . . especially when he had added some salt to it.

5. The After-Soup Announcement

I don't suppose, said Grimble to himself, that we need have a very large turkey, but it ought to be a turkey. A pigeon put under his father's microscope might look all right, but he was sure it wouldn't taste the same.

At breakfast his father was in a very good mood. They ate a lot of streaky bacon, which his father cooked under the grill because that way the fat ran off and the bacon became crisp, and you can eat it with your fingers. Also they read the papers. FATHER CHRISTMAS HITS CHILD IN CHEMIST SHOP said the headline in one of them.

"What on earth was Father Christmas *doing* in a chemist shop?" asked Grimble.

"There are two things," said his father. "Either he had a headache and was getting an aspirin, or he was stocking up with talcum powder. Nearly everyone gets talcum powder. It is one of the most giving things there is, so Father Christmas needs a lot of it."

"Does he make his own?" asked Grimble.

"This is a silly conversation," said his father. "What happened to Chelsea?"

"I do not wish to know that," said Grimble. "What is happening to Plymouth Argyle?"

They left a very neat pile of washing-up for Mrs Grimble who had gone to bed with her feet again, and Mr Grimble said "Come into the study . . . I want to talk to you."

Grimble tucked his shirt, which usually hung outside his trousers, back into his trousers and followed his father into the study. "Sit down," said Mr Grimble. It sounded quite an important meeting, so Grimble rubbed his shoes against the back of his socks to polish them and sat down.

"Well now," said his father, "I have news for you. Next Wednesday is Christmas Day."

"I know that," said Grimble. "I have known that all winter."

"Please let me continue. Next Wednesday is Christmas Day and today we are going to go to a restaurant for lunch. Do you understand?"

Grimble said he understood both things his father had said. But even if they went to the best restaurant anywhere and ate everything that restaurant sold, he would still be very hungry by next Wednesday. Unlike camels, who had a drink and could make it last for a week, human beings had to be fed daily.

"At this luncheon," said his father, ignoring Grimble, "I shall make an important announcement concerning the whole Grimble family and Christmas."

"Isn't it possible to tell me what it is now?" asked

Grimble. "You see I have been worrying quite a lot about Christmas and lunch time is still hours away."

His father shook his head. "All I can tell you is that the news will be announced directly after the soup."

"Suppose we have grapefruit instead?" asked Grimble.

"No soup, no news," said his father and started twisting the globe of the world. "Second time today I have lost the Falkland Islands," he muttered. "Ah there they are. Just to the right of Patagonia," and he got a magnifying glass and examined them carefully.

Grimble went out partly happy because he liked restaurants but partly worried because he did like to know exactly what was going to happen, when it was going to happen . . . and an important family announcement after the soup was a bit too vague for comfort. Grimble found his encyclopedia and looked up turkey. "Turkey" . . . said the book: "Republican country lying partly in Asia and partly in Europe." As this was not the turkey he had in mind he looked up the next column and it said: "Turkey – large game bird with a pendent dilatable appendage on the head and a wrinkled and tuberculed neck. The male weighs up to 34 pounds." He did not understand that – except the weight part.

As the encyclopedia did not give the price, he went down the street to the butcher's shop, where there were a lot of turkeys in the window with THIS JOINT cards stuck into them and every THIS JOINT card had a price written on it.

The small turkeys cost at least two pounds fifty pence and some of the bigger ones cost much more than that. For a boy who had 119p, some tree delivery money, and an Irish 5p piece it was quite obvious that this was too expensive. With a swift decision such as Nelson, Napoleon and other

52

leaders have had to make in their time, Grimble made up his mind: *No turkey from me to the old Grimbles.* They cost too much and it's not really my job . . . anyway the announcement after the soup might well make the whole idea of turkey-buying unnecessary.

On the other hand . . . on the other hand I have five fingers . . . that was David Sebastian Waghorn's joke . . . (David Sebastian Waghorn was a very funny boy.)

On the other hand he had not yet bought any real Christmas presents for his parents – the fudge he had made for them was all right but he had used *their* sugar and *their* milk and *their* chocolate so it was really more their present to them.

119p is a fair amount of money to spend on presents for two people so perhaps he could keep his earnings from the Christmas trees for himself. He thought about it and decided he should spend 79p on his father and 40p on his mother. Then he thought that was a bit mean; his mother had been very good to him about the welsh rarebits, so he made it 69 and 50. His mother ought to have something for her feet and his father some arrows that would stick to the globe, so that he could find places again when he was looking for them.

He went into a stationer's shop and there were some good red stick-on arrows in an envelope that cost 19p, and as this left exactly 50p and the shop sold a book called *Grimble* by Clement Freud for 25p, he bought two. He thought it was a jolly good name for a book.

For his mother he bought four 12½p tins of talcum powder, one smelling of lavender, one of violets, one of roses and one of French fern. They did not have any onion talcum powder. He asked and the chemist said not.

Back in the Grimble household, preparations for going out to the restaurant were in full swing. Mr Grimble had put a dust sheet over his globe, combed his hair, and put on a pair of purple socks. As neither of the Grimbles drove a car (in fact the Grimbles did not have a car) a taxi had been ordered to take them to the bus stop. It was going to be a really proper outing.

The restaurant to which the Grimbles went was called The French Restaurant. All the waiters were Italian and the chef was Indian. He sometimes came in and watched people eat to make sure they did not leave anything on their plates, and when they had finished he would turn to the waiters and say, "There, I was right."

A man with a long finger came up to the Grimbles and said, "Follow my finger," and he held it up and they followed it to a table. Then the man gave them a menu and went away.

After a while he came back with a piece of paper and a pencil, to write down what they had chosen to eat. Grimble ordered vegetable soup and some roast chicken and bacon and fried onion and spinach. His parents said prawn cocktail and duck, both of them. He thought that was a waste. If they were both going to have the same things, they could have had it at home. Restaurants were for being different in.

When he had finished his soup and his father had finally got hold of the last prawn in the cocktail glass and swallowed it, he gave a small cough and said, "Here is the Christmas announcement. At half past three tomorrow afternoon the Grimble household will leave for Africa by taxi and bus and then by train and boat. We shall spend Christmas on the SS *Particular*, which is a very luxurious kind of passenger ship with nine out of ten for roast turkey and the best Christmas-pudding maker in the Mediterranean Sea. I expect you have heard of *Particular* Christmas pudding."

"On Boxing Day we arrive in Ifni, which is at the top end of the Sahara desert and we will take sand samples, which I need very badly for my work. We will then fly home."

"In an aeroplane?" asked Grimble.

"I have always felt that to be the best way to fly," said his father.

The chicken and the duck then arrived and the waiter got all the vegetables wrong.

"It is going to be an absolutely marvellous Christmas," said Grimble. "It is going to be the best Christmas I have ever had, I know it is."

"There are," said his father, "one or two things I feel I should tell you. While the good ship *Particular*'s chef is a master in the art of making Christmas puddings he has absolutely no idea about the manufacture of Christmas cake. I should have bought a Christmas cake and taken it with us – but I regret that it is now too late. It is very sad, but I only thought about this on the bus."

Grimble turned a bit red and said, "It so happens that I have a Christmas cake ready and iced and rather looking forward to going to Africa."

His parents looked at him with great admiration.

"It also happens," said Grimble, "that my presents to you are very small and light and they will be most suitable to be brought back on an aeroplane."

They munched their chicken and duck and as the old Grimbles picked up their pieces of duck in their fingers, Grimble realized that this would be an all right thing to do; after all it was a *French* restaurant.

When he had pulled the wishbone with his father . . . and lost – his father was very pleased – he said to his mother, "If we are going to Africa, why did you buy a Christmas tree?"

"Against burglars," said his mother. "If a burglar sees a Christmas tree in a house he knows there is someone in and does not burgle anything."

"Why did you hide the tree in the shed then?"

"Well, we don't want the burglars to know everything," said his mother.

"And the cardboard box," said Grimble, "the one we brought home from the shops. What was in that?"

"Washing powder," said his mother, "2p off."

Grimble ordered ice cream, but as he had eaten too much soup and chicken and onions he could not finish the ice cream, so the Italian waiter said, "As it is very near Christmas let me wrap it up and put in some more and you can take it home and have it for tea."

It really was going to be a super Christmas.